The Heart's Song

Gilles Tibo

Illustrated by

Irene Luxbacher

North Winds Press
An Imprint of Scholastic Canada Ltd.

For all the Miss Matildas of this world.
— G.T.

For Luca, Isabella, Noah and Elijah, with love.
— I.L.

The artwork for this book was rendered in acrylics, graphite,
charcoal and found papers and assembled digitally.

Library and Archives Canada Cataloguing in Publication

Tibo, Gilles, 1951-
[Grand coeur de Madame Lili. English]
The heart's song / Gilles Tibo ; illustrated by Irene Luxbacher ; translated
by Petra Johannson.

ISBN 978-1-4431-5721-6 (hardcover)

I. Luxbacher, Irene, 1970-, illustrator II. Johannson, Petra, translator
III. Title. IV. Title: Grand coeur de Madame Lili. English.

PS8589.I26G6713 2017   jC843'.54   C2017-901617-2

www.scholastic.ca

6 5 4 3 2 1   Printed in Malaysia 108   17 18 19 20 21

Every morning, Miss Matilda woke to her canary's sweet song. The beautiful music filled her heart with joy as she got ready for the day.

Then she said goodbye to her little bird and left the house, pulling a large suitcase behind her. A stranger might think Miss Matilda was leaving for a long trip, but everyone who knew her knew just where she was going.

It wasn't to the train station or the airport. Miss Matilda was going to the park. There she greeted everyone by name, then sat on her favourite bench near the sandbox.

The children brought her their broken toys: a truck with a wobbly wheel, a broken doll, a bucket with a hole.

Miss Matilda would open her suitcase. Inside were perfect rows of shiny tools: hammers, pliers, screwdrivers of all shapes and sizes.

On sunny days, Miss Matilda repaired toys, and sunglasses, parasols and sun hats. On cloudy days, she fixed toys, and rubber boots, raincoats and umbrellas.

She also had tools to mend rips in pants, holey socks and shoes that needed repair.

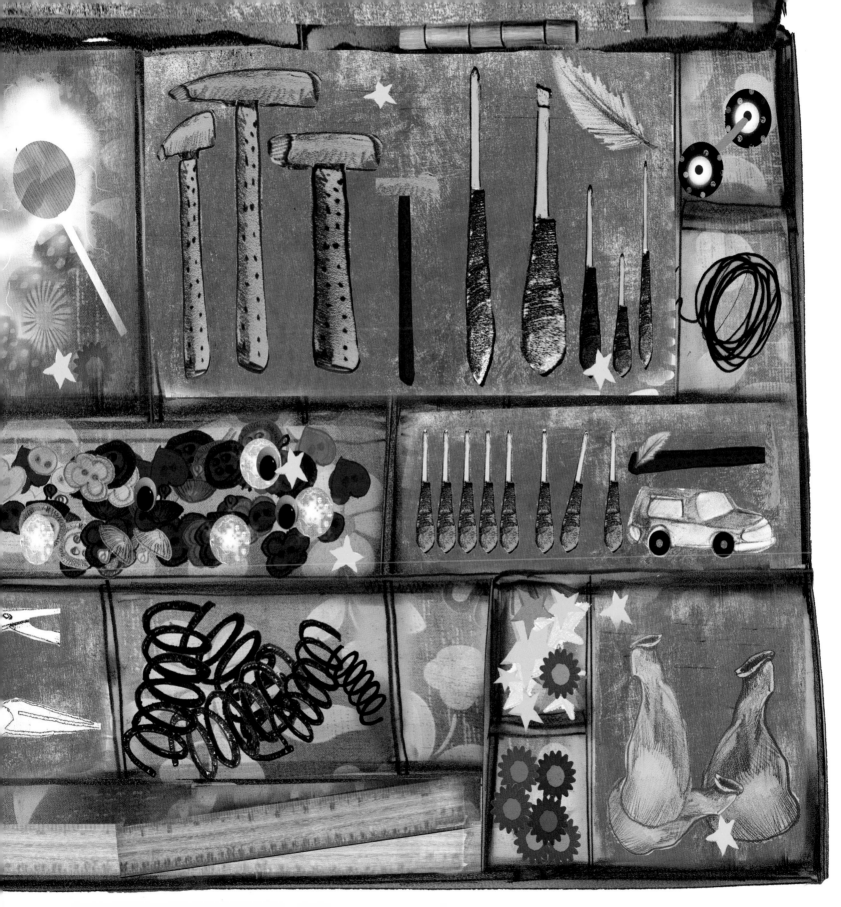

One day, Miss Matilda was fixing a stuffed bear when she heard crying. Jeremy was curled up under the swings. Miss Matilda checked his legs, his arms, his neck, but he wasn't injured.

Still Jeremy kept crying, and Miss Matilda finally understood. His hurt could not be seen.

Miss Matilda opened her suitcase and searched for the right tool: A screwdriver? A bandage? A spool of thread? There was nothing.

At last, Miss Matilda closed her suitcase and knelt beside Jeremy. As he cried, she sang a lullaby. She sang so softly his tears stopped, and she kept singing until he closed his eyes and fell asleep.

They stayed that way for a long time. Whenever a child came to her with a broken toy, she whispered, "Come back later, dear. Right now, I'm mending a broken heart."

When Jeremy woke up, he kissed Miss Matilda on the cheek. Then he ran back to the swing. Soon, his laughter seemed to soar all the way up to the sun.

From that day on, as she listened to her canary in the morning, Miss Matilda wrote new melodies in a songbook she kept in her suitcase.

From her park bench, she still repaired toys, but people also brought her other hurts to heal.

One day, she comforted a girl who had lost her cat.

Another day, a boy who wanted his dad to come home.

She consoled a girl who longed for a friend.

She sang to a boy who missed his grandmother, and a girl who didn't want to move away.

And then one morning, Miss Matilda arrived at the park without her case of tools. Her eyes were filled with tears.

All the children, and their mothers, fathers and babysitters, surrounded her. Miss Matilda told them that her little canary would never sing again.

From her coat pocket, she tenderly removed
a small bundle wrapped in a silk scarf.

She gazed at it and let the tears roll down
her cheeks.

The hours went by and people left the park to return to their busy lives. Miss Matilda stayed on the bench, alone with her sadness.

As the sun began to set, Miss Matilda heard a sound. When she looked up, all the children were coming toward her, each one holding a suitcase, their voices joined together in song.

The children opened their bags. One after another, they unfolded beautiful pictures, poems and messages of love.

Miss Matilda's face lit up as she studied each gift. She knew she would never forget her little yellow bird, but her heart was filled with joy.